Dear Parent:
Your child's love of reading starts here!

Every child learns to read in a different way and at his or her own speed. Some go back and forth between reading levels and read favorite books again and again. Others read through each level in order. You can help your young reader improve and become more confident by encouraging his or her own interests and abilities. From books your child reads with you to the first books he or she reads alone, there are I Can Read Books for every stage of reading:

SHARED READING
Basic language, word repetition, and whimsical illustrations, ideal for sharing with your emergent reader

BEGINNING READING
Short sentences, familiar words, and simple concepts for children eager to read on their own

READING WITH HELP
Engaging stories, longer sentences, and language play for developing readers

READING ALONE
Complex plots, challenging vocabulary, and high-interest topics for the independent reader

I Can Read Books have introduced children to the joy of reading since 1957. Featuring award-winning authors and illustrators and a fabulous cast of beloved characters, I Can Read Books set the standard for beginning readers.

A lifetime of discovery begins with the magical words "I Can Read!"

*Visit www.icanread.com for information
on enriching your child's reading experience.*

For Olivia and Ryan,
friends of the tooth fairy!
—H. P.

For McKenzie, with love!
—L. A.

The art was created digitally in Adobe Photoshop®.

I Can Read® and I Can Read Book® are trademarks of HarperCollins Publishers.
Amelia Bedelia is a registered trademark of Peppermint Partners, LLC.

Library of Congress Cataloging-in-Publication Data
Names: Parish, Herman, author. | Avril, Lynne, illustrator.
Title: Amelia Bedelia lost and found / by Herman Parish ; pictures by Lynne Avril.
Other titles: Lost and found
Description: First edition. | New York, NY : Greenwillow Books, an Imprint of HarperCollins Publishers, [2020] | Audience: Ages 4-8. | Audience: Grades K-1. | Summary: "Amelia Bedelia loses her tooth . . . and then she loses it again. But it's finders keepers in the end"—Provided by publisher.
Identifiers: LCCN 2019054627 | ISBN 9780062961969 (paperback) | ISBN 9780062961976 (hardcover) | ISBN 9780062961983 (ebook)
Subjects: CYAC: Teeth—Fiction. | Lost and found possessions—Fiction. | Schools—Fiction. | Humorous stories.
Classification: LCC PZ7.P2185 Aow 2020 | DDC [E]—dc23
LC record available at https://lccn.loc.gov/2019054627

20 21 22 23 24 LSCC 10 9 8 7 6 5 4 3 2 1   ❖   First Edition
Greenwillow Books

I Can Read!

1 BEGINNING READING

Amelia Bedelia

·Lost and Found·

by Herman Parish ✿ pictures by Lynne Avril

Greenwillow Books, *An Imprint of* HarperCollins*Publishers*

Amelia Bedelia wiggled her loose tooth.

She pushed it back and forth.

She pushed it side to side.

It was a losing battle.

No matter what Amelia Bedelia did,

her tooth would not fall out.

"Let me yank it out for you,"
said Amelia Bedelia's father.
"Your tooth is hanging by a thread,"
said Amelia Bedelia's mother.
"It will come out by itself."
Amelia Bedelia looked in the mirror.
She did not see a thread.

Amelia Bedelia was getting worried.

What if her tooth came out

when she was eating?

What if she swallowed it?

Then she could not put it under

her pillow for the Tooth Fairy.

Amelia Bedelia wiggled her loose tooth
at school.

"I lost my tooth at the beach,"
said Holly. "A wave knocked it out."
"I got hit by a Frisbee," said Skip.
"Mine got stuck in a brownie," said Joy.

Amelia Bedelia poked Skip

with a pencil.

"Here is your pencil back," she said.

Skip spun around.

His elbow bumped her mouth.

"OWWWWWW!" yelled Amelia Bedelia.

"I am sorry," said Skip.

"It was an accident."

Amelia Bedelia covered her mouth
with her hands.

She jumped up and down.

She did a little dance.

When Amelia Bedelia sat down again

her friends gasped.

"You look different," said Rose.

"Your tooth is gone!" said Joy.

It was true.

Amelia Bedelia stuck
her tongue through the gap
where her loose tooth had been.
She felt lost without it!

"I lost my tooth," said Amelia Bedelia.
"Bravo!" said Miss Edwards, her
teacher. "Where did you lose it?"
Amelia Bedelia pointed
at the gap in her teeth.

"Where did it go?" asked Miss Edwards.

Amelia Bedelia looked around.

"I lost it," she said.

"I hope it is not your sweet tooth,"
said Miss Edwards.

Dawn crawled under

Amelia Bedelia's desk.

"Here it is," she said.

"Thank you," said Amelia Bedelia.

Miss Edwards gave
Amelia Bedelia
a tiny box.

Amelia Bedelia dropped her tooth into it.

She snapped the little box shut.

Amelia Bedelia shook the box

back and forth.

She heard her tooth rattle.

Clickity—CLICK—click.

Clickity
Click
Click

Amelia Bedelia learned to eat her lunch
with one less tooth.

She learned to drink her milk
with one less tooth.
It felt funny!

Amelia Bedelia opened and closed

the tiny box again and again.

She showed her tooth to all her friends.

19

Art class was after lunch.

Amelia Bedelia wanted

to paint a picture of her lost tooth.

She opened the box.

Her tooth was gone!

"I lost my tooth,"

said Amelia Bedelia to Skip.

"I know. I knocked it out," said Skip.

"I just lost the tooth I lost,"

said Amelia Bedelia.

"You lost your tooth again?" said Skip.

Amelia Bedelia nodded.

"I will help you find it," said Skip.

"I have nothing to lose."

Amelia Bedelia and Skip

looked in the cafeteria.

The cafeteria had been cleaned.

The tables were spotless.

The floors were shining.

"Maybe someone took your tooth

to the Lost and Found," said Skip.

Amelia Bedelia and Skip

ran to the school office.

"Where did you lose your tooth?"

said Mr. Rice, the principal.

"If I knew where I lost it,"

said Amelia Bedelia,

"it would not be lost."

"Follow me," said Mr. Rice.

"I've lost count of all the things

in the Lost and Found."

Amelia Bedelia spotted a mitten.

"Hey, that is my mitten," she said.

"I lost it a long time ago."

She tried it on.

"It still fits," she said.

"Check out this cool stuff," said Skip.

He bounced a rubber ball on the floor.

He lost his grip.

The ball smacked a shelf

of tiny treasures.

Clickity—CLICK—click.

Something small hit the floor.

"My tooth!" said Amelia Bedelia. "Finders keepers, losers weepers," said Mr. Rice. "You are lucky!" Amelia Bedelia put her tooth back in the box and shut it tight. SNAP!

"You lost your tooth two times,"
said Skip.
"Maybe the tooth fairy
will leave you two times as much."

That night, Amelia Bedelia
tucked her tooth under her pillow.
In her dreams
the tooth fairy sang,
"Lost and found
and lost and found."

31

When Amelia Bedelia woke up,

she looked under her pillow.

Her tooth was gone,

but this time it was not lost.

"Finders keepers!" said Amelia Bedelia.

Dear Parent:

Congratulations! Your child is taking the first steps on an exciting journey. The destination? Independent reading!

STEP INTO READING® will help your child get there. The program offers five steps to reading success. Each step includes fun stories and colorful art. There are also Step into Reading Sticker Books, Step into Reading Math Readers, Step into Reading Phonics Readers, Step into Reading Write-In Readers, and Step into Reading Phonics Boxed Sets—a complete literacy program with something to interest every child.

Learning to Read, Step by Step!

Ready to Read   Preschool–Kindergarten
• **big type and easy words** • **rhyme and rhythm** • **picture clues**
For children who know the alphabet and are eager to begin reading.

Reading with Help   Preschool–Grade 1
• **basic vocabulary** • **short sentences** • **simple stories**
For children who recognize familiar words and sound out new words with help.

Reading on Your Own   Grades 1–3
• **engaging characters** • **easy-to-follow plots** • **popular topics**
For children who are ready to read on their own.

Reading Paragraphs   Grades 2–3
• **challenging vocabulary** • **short paragraphs** • **exciting stories**
For newly independent readers who read simple sentences with confidence.

Ready for Chapters   Grades 2–4
• **chapters** • **longer paragraphs** • **full-color art**
For children who want to take the plunge into chapter books but still like colorful pictures.

STEP INTO READING® is designed to give every child a successful reading experience. The grade levels are only guides. Children can progress through the steps at their own speed, developing confidence in their reading, no matter what their grade.

Remember, a lifetime love of reading starts with a single step!

For my brave little girls,
Lilly and Lucy
—M.L.

Visit us on the Web!
StepIntoReading.com
randomhouse.com/kids

Educators and librarians, for a variety of teaching tools, visit us at
randomhouse.com/teachers

ISBN: 978-0-7364-2916-0 (trade) — ISBN: 978-0-7364-8109-0 (lib. bdg.)

Printed in the United States of America   10 9 8 7 6 5 4 3